Sometimes our mind lets go of memories because it considers them insignificant.

Sometimes it buries them deep, to protect us.

But at some point, we're ready to face our greatest fears, and the memories resurface.

R.W. WALLACE

Author of the Ghost Detective Series

HIDDEN HORRORS

A Mystery Short Story

Hidden Horrors
by R.W. Wallace

Copyright © 2020 by R.W. Wallace

Copy editing by Jinxie Gervasio
Cover by the author
Cover Illustration 39657317 © sondem | 123rf.com

All characters and events in this book, other than those clearly in the public domain, are fictitious and any resemblance to real persons, living or dead, is purely coincidental.

All rights reserved. No part of this publication may be reproduced, distributed, or transmitted in any form or by any means, including photocopying, recording, or other electronic or mechanical methods, without the prior written permission of the publisher, except in the case of brief quotations embodied in critical reviews and certain other noncommercial uses permitted by copyright law. For permission requests, write to the publisher, addressed "Attention: Permissions Coordinator," at the address below.

www.rwwallace.com

ISBN: [979-10-95707-44-8]

Main category—Fiction
Other category—Mystery

First Edition

14 13 12 11 10 / 10 9 8 7 6 5 4 3 2 1

Also by R.W. Wallace

Mystery

The Tolosa Mystery Series
The Red Brick Haze (free)
The Red Brick Cellars
The Red Brick Basilica

Ghost Detective Shorts (coming soon)
Just Desserts
Lost Friends
Family Bonds
Till Death
Common Ground

Short Stories
Cold Blue Eternity
Critters
Gertrude and the Trojan Horse
First Impressions
Let Them Eat Cake
Out of Sight
Two's Company
Like Mother Like Daughter

Science Fiction (short stories)
The Vanguard

Lollapalooza Shorts
Quarantine
Common Enemies

Adventure (short stories)
Size Matters

Fantasy (short stories)
Morbier Impossible
Unexpected Consequences

ONE

Take a deep breath in through the nose. Out through the mouth.

I inhale deeply. The smell of figs reach me through the open window, even though the compost is at the far end of the garden. My husband Marc spent the afternoon raking below the fig tree and the smell of ripe fruit is going to be an integral part of our back yard for a while.

My pantry is filling up with pots of jam. When I reached twenty pots, I decided we had enough to last our family of four until next year. The last batch of figs went into a pie, and the rest I hereby offer to the blackbirds and the wasps.

On the next breath, gently close your eyes and let your breathing go back to normal.

Dammit, my mind wandered again. I follow the instructions and let my eyes close.

Open your senses. Feel your contact with your surroundings. Sounds. Smells.

Well, my ass is firmly planted on my chair and I'm feeling nice and heavy. The murmur of the cars from the highway is fairly faint today, like it always is on a heavy and humid summer night. The neighbors are having a party again, but it's not too noisy. Just some chatting between friends and some low-key music. Madame Humbert next door keeps complaining about them every time we meet. She apparently feels that owning a house in a somewhat rich neighborhood should protect you against anyone below the age of twenty-five. Too bad the neighbor decided he'd rent out his house to a group of five students.

A gentle smile touches my lips. I happen to like the youngsters. Makes the backyard feel alive and fun. Almost magical in its calmness.

Now bring your focus to your breath.

Aaaah! Meditation. I'm meditating, not judging my neighbors. I'm never going to get the hang of this.

I focus on my breath. I know how to do this. Chest rising, stomach growing. Chest lowering, stomach back in. Rinse and repeat.

The guy on the meditation app doesn't always say the same thing, but a couple of sessions ago, he mentioned imagining swinging back and forth in your mind. It certainly helped me staying focused on the breath and not go off on tangents every thirty seconds.

So I imagine myself on a swing. I breathe in and I swing forward. I breathe out and I swing backward. I feel the wind in my hair, log brown strands flapping in my eyes on the return. I'm wearing a pink sun dress—I think it's my favorite from when I was five years old.

In my mind, I'm five-year-old me, swinging from the branches of the apple tree in my parents' garden, smiling from ear to ear.

I can see the butterflies, feel the sun on my face. Hear my mother calling in the background.

I tighten my hold on the ropes and lean back so I'm horizontal on the forward swing. More wind. Going higher.

Smiling wider.

This feels so good. Gone is the stress from work. I'm not wondering if my daughter has done her homework. I'm not feeling guilty about not having cleaned the downstairs bathroom like I'd planned. My only goal is to go higher, faster.

At the top of my curve, as I start to breathe out, I'm weightless. My dress floats around me and I'm frozen in space for just a second.

Then I breathe out and I swing back.

Next breath in, and I lean into it again. This time, when I reach the top, it feels like the swing is holding me back.

What happens if I let go?

I continue my meditation, breathing in and out, leaning into the swing on every breath in. *Can* I let go? Could that be the point of the meditation? To just let everything go?

The guy on the app talks, something about not worrying if the mind wanders, but I'm tuning him out. I keep swinging, keep reliving details from my childhood.

I hear my mother's voice again. She's telling me she's going to take a shower.

I haven't heard her voice in over thirty years. In fact, I can't quite remember the very last time I heard it, though I know I was five. One thing I do remember is fighting with my dad because I wanted to wear the pink sun dress to the funeral, but he wouldn't let me.

I'm still leaning into every swing and my butt is leaving the swing at the top of every curve. Only my hands on the ropes are holding me back.

I used to love jumping off the swing at top speed.

When did I stop doing that?

I decide *to hell with it*. On the next breath in, I lean into the swing with all my might. But instead of holding on at the top—I let go.

I'm flying.

Pink dress around my ears. Feet toward the sky. Arms flailing.

I land with a *thump*.

God, this feels real. I've lost all contact with my body sitting in a chair in my bedroom at home. All I can feel is the need to *breathe*. Where did all the air go?

I roll over on my side and realize I'm lying in the grass. Some ten meters away I see the old swing moving lazily back and forth now that I'm no longer there to boost it, sunlight dappling the wooden seat as it shines through the leaves of the apple tree.

I still can't draw breath. My brain knows it'll come back eventually, but my body's still panicking.

I remember this. It's not a memory I ever think about, but this really happened. I was wearing my pretty dress and wanted to watch it as I flew through the air. But I miscalculated and let go too late, so I didn't manage to land on my feet.

Finally, I manage to draw a breath.

Then push it right back out in an ear-splitting scream.

My arm's hurting. Now that my lungs are working again, the rest of my body's letting itself be known.

Though I'm feeling the pain and the panic of my little body, I'm also observing as an adult. I'm watching five-year-old me crying and screaming for her mother because she's in pain and she's scared.

I miss knowing that I have someone who'll always come when I call for help.

Mom doesn't disappoint. Seconds after my scream, she comes hurtling out the kitchen door, wearing nothing but a pair of white panties and a pink bra. She must have been on her way into the shower.

She sprints across the lawn and kneels at my side, putting her hands on both sides of my face. "Where does it hurt, honey? What happened?"

I realize I'm still screaming. Mom manages to get her questions in when I draw breath. I will myself to stop, but I have no power over what's going on. I'm only along for the ride as a passenger.

I'm somehow reliving a memory from my childhood that I'd completely forgotten about. But now that I see it, I know it really happened. I know traumatic incidents can cause memory loss, but a broken arm doesn't feel like it should be traumatic enough.

"I don't think it's broken, honey," Mom says. She's figured out it's the arm that's the problem and has gently rolled me to the side so she can inspect it. "Maybe sprained something, but there's no blood. Can you move your fingers for me?"

I'm still screaming, but by shorter bouts, and with less volume. It seems like the thing to do when you're suffering.

I move my fingers and Mom rewards me with a huge smile.

"See? Not broken." She caresses my cheek with one hand. "But I realize it's hurting, honey. Do you think you can walk up to the house? I just need to get dressed, then we'll go to see the doctor so he can heal it."

But five-year-old me doesn't think I can get up. Even the idea of moving around is making me go back to the original blood-curdling screams.

"Don't cry, baby," Mom coos. "I'll carry you in."

"Do you need any help, Ma'am?" a male voice says from the street.

My mother freezes and glances down at her mostly naked body. There's a hedge separating our garden from the street, but it's not very high—well, it is for five-year-old me, but not for adults—and anyone can just step through.

Five year-old me doesn't think much about my mother looking down at herself, except to note that her bra is the exact same beautiful pink as my dress, but adult me cringes at finding yourself half naked in front of a stranger. Depending on the person on the other side of the hedge, they could even sue for public indecency if they were so inclined.

Mom's chest is heaving rapidly and her face is very pale. My continued screaming probably isn't helping. Clenching her teeth together, she raises her head to face the stranger. "My daughter fell and hurt her arm," she says calmly.

"Can I be of assistance?" I can't see the man since my eyes are focused solely on Mom, but his voice is calm and polite. At least it doesn't sound like he'll go after her for walking around in plain view in her underwear.

Mom hesitates. But I'd always been on the big side and she'd been refusing to carry me for over a year already. With a broken or sprained arm to boot, it was mission impossible.

"Would you mind helping me carry her to the house?" she asks.

"Of course." I hear the rustling of someone pushing through the hedge and then he comes to stand in my field of vision, right behind my mother. He has dark blond hair, brown eyes, and a nose that's too small for his face. His lips are a little on the thin side, but they lift into a smile as he looks at me.

Then the smile turns decidedly lecherous as he lets his eyes wander down my mother's back while she has her back turned.

Five-year-old me only thinks he must be admiring the pretty pink like I did, but adult me has a cold finger running down my spine. I want to tell her to make the man go away, to tell him she'll manage on her own.

I try to stop screaming, but I'm not the one deciding what's going on here today. Five-year-old me is still hurting, so she's still screaming.

Mom turns to talk to the man and his face is all polite again. "Could you lift her while I hold her arm?" she asks.

"Of course." The man leans down and slides one arm under my torso and the other under my knees. He lifts me up like I'm nothing but a teddy bear while Mom follows the movement, making sure my arm isn't jostled.

When they're both standing, Mom's face is just above my own. Which means that the man must be towering above her.

Adult me would be having a galloping heart, if I still had a body to manage. But try as I might to take over the little girl's body, I'm clearly only a passenger.

Mom leads the man across the lawn and toward the kitchen door. "Thank you so much for your help..." She glances up at him, hesitation in her eyes.

"George," he says. "George Lambert."

Mom nods. "Thank you, George. I can't remember seeing you around these parts?"

Good on you, Mom. She seems to have caught on to the guy not being the cleanest guy out there—or it was just her feeling vulnerable because she was bringing a guy into her house while wearing nothing but her underwear.

George smiles, but it doesn't reach his eyes. "It's the first time I come to this neighborhood, Ma'am. I design bathrooms and have a meeting with one of your neighbors in thirty minutes.

I prefer to see the old one with my own eyes before giving an estimate."

We reach the kitchen and Mom points to one of the chairs. "Would you mind setting her down there, please?"

George deposits me on the chair and I throw my arms around Mom—including the hurt one, proving it isn't all that hurt—and downgrade the screams to hulks.

As Mom whispers reassurances into my ear, I watch George watching us. Ankles crossed, he leans against the kitchen counter as he leisurely admires my mother's behind again. He glances at his watch, then back to my mother's body, then out the window, where he has a panoramic view of our entire street.

"You'll be fine, honey," my mother tells me as she rubs my back. "Mom just needs to go get dressed, all right? Can you stay here with the nice man for one minute while I go get some pants and a t-shirt?"

Adult me heaves a relieved breath as five-year-old me hold on tighter around Mom's neck.

How can I not know what's going to happen? As the events run their course, the memories resurface. I *know* this actually happened. But I have no idea what's going to happen in a second, or in a minute, or in an hour.

And I don't like it. Any of it. Fear is burning in my stomach and I'm unable to tell which version of me is doing that.

Perhaps it's both.

George pushes away from the counter and comes to stand next to my mother. Adult me figures this gives him a perfect view of her cleavage.

He brushes a hand through my hair. "Don't worry, kiddo. We'll be fine for a minute, won't we?"

Mom's gaze zeroes in on his hand. The tiniest of lines appears between her eyebrows. "Actually," she says, her voice falsely light, "I can get dressed after we take care of the arm."

She forces my arms off her neck, making my hulks go back to screams, and gets up to face George. "Thank you so much for your help, George. I can take it from here." When he makes no move to leave, she adds, "Perhaps you'd like to leave through the front door, so you don't need to go through the hedge again?"

George lets his gaze run slowly from my mother's head to her toes. "Actually," he says and lifts a hand to run along one of her bra's pink straps. "I think I'd like to stay a little longer. You don't resist and I promise not to touch the kid."

I prefer to see the old one with my own eyes before giving an estimate."

We reach the kitchen and Mom points to one of the chairs. "Would you mind setting her down there, please?"

George deposits me on the chair and I throw my arms around Mom—including the hurt one, proving it isn't all that hurt—and downgrade the screams to hulks.

As Mom whispers reassurances into my ear, I watch George watching us. Ankles crossed, he leans against the kitchen counter as he leisurely admires my mother's behind again. He glances at his watch, then back to my mother's body, then out the window, where he has a panoramic view of our entire street.

"You'll be fine, honey," my mother tells me as she rubs my back. "Mom just needs to go get dressed, all right? Can you stay here with the nice man for one minute while I go get some pants and a t-shirt?"

Adult me heaves a relieved breath as five-year-old me hold on tighter around Mom's neck.

How can I not know what's going to happen? As the events run their course, the memories resurface. I *know* this actually happened. But I have no idea what's going to happen in a second, or in a minute, or in an hour.

And I don't like it. Any of it. Fear is burning in my stomach and I'm unable to tell which version of me is doing that.

Perhaps it's both.

George pushes away from the counter and comes to stand next to my mother. Adult me figures this gives him a perfect view of her cleavage.

He brushes a hand through my hair. "Don't worry, kiddo. We'll be fine for a minute, won't we?"

Mom's gaze zeroes in on his hand. The tiniest of lines appears between her eyebrows. "Actually," she says, her voice falsely light, "I can get dressed after we take care of the arm."

She forces my arms off her neck, making my hulks go back to screams, and gets up to face George. "Thank you so much for your help, George. I can take it from here." When he makes no move to leave, she adds, "Perhaps you'd like to leave through the front door, so you don't need to go through the hedge again?"

George lets his gaze run slowly from my mother's head to her toes. "Actually," he says and lifts a hand to run along one of her bra's pink straps. "I think I'd like to stay a little longer. You don't resist and I promise not to touch the kid."

Two

I NEVER KNEW the details around my mother's death. I knew she'd been murdered and I knew they'd never found the killer.

The first times I'd asked my father, he'd say I was too young. He kept the information from me to protect me.

As I grew older, I realized that me asking the question hurt *him*. Made him even more distant. So I stopped asking. I cherished the memories I had of Mom and came to terms with the fact that my mother was a cold case.

A couple of times, the police came to talk to my dad. The last time was when I was twenty-eight and home on vacation, and this time I was considered adult enough to listen in. They'd discovered some new method for doing DNA tests and wanted

Dad's authorization to do new checks on the little evidence they'd gathered at the murder scene.

They actually had the DNA. That wasn't the problem. The problem was that the killer wasn't in any of the databases.

Still, Dad always agreed to let them reopen the case. Before going back to staring at the wall.

Even then, once the police had left, I didn't ask my dad about the circumstances of Mom's death. I figured the reason he didn't want to give me the details was that he didn't know them himself.

I never realized it was because I *did* know them.

Three

THERE'S BLOOD *EVERYWHERE*.

The kitchen's covered in it. I'm not really taking in any other details, though. I understand why I suppressed these memories, why I can't remember my Mom's last words. It's just too horrific.

I'm still screaming. This time, I'm in complete agreement with my five-year-old self, and help her along to keep screaming, even when the voice is gone and it can't really qualify for anything but hissing.

She never closes her eyes, so I see everything.

When it's all over, George stands above me, panting. His clothes are covered in my mother's blood.

I look up at him, wondering what he'll do. I don't remember it—I still only remember things as they happen—but I'm not actually afraid he'll hurt me. I'm still alive, aren't I?

It gives me the calmness I need to continue observing. Five-year-old me isn't so lucky.

"Time to stop screaming, kid," he says. He sits down on his haunches to come face to face with me. His hair is covered in blood, his chin has a deep gouge—this is where the DNA they found under Mom's fingernails would have come from—and his pupils are so dilated I can barely make out the brown of the iris.

"Stop screaming or I'll hurt you."

The screaming stops. Hiccups start up instead, but George doesn't seem to mind.

"You're not going to tell anyone about this, are you?" His eyelids are heavy as he studies me. He oozes confidence, as if he's not worried in the least of getting caught.

I expect my head to start shaking, but nothing happens. Just another hiccup.

"What's your name, kiddo?" he asks.

No reply.

"Give me a nod and I'll let you go to your room."

Still nothing.

One side of his thin lips lift in a satisfied smile and he slaps his hands on his bloody knees, pushing off to get back up.

I just sit there and watch as he gets ready to leave. He takes his time about it, too. He goes to the bathroom to take a shower. He takes a plastic bag and shoves all his dirty clothes inside. He left the door open, so I can see him from my spot in the kitchen.

He has a birthmark on the back of his upper thigh—it's three overlapping circles and they make me think of Mickey Mouse.

He goes to my parents' room and I hear him rummaging around in the closet. Five minutes later, he emerges wearing one of my Dad's suits. It's a bit short in the legs, but it's not obvious he's wearing another man's clothes.

He grabs the plastic bag, and without so much as a backward glance at me or my mother, throws out a carefree, "Later, kiddo," before slamming the kitchen door shut behind him. I see him jumping the hedge at the back of the garden, leading to a small wood that I'd never been to because my parents judged it too dangerous.

Four

I sit there, in my five-year-old body, for what feels like an eternity. How long is this trip down memory lane supposed to last? Until I catch up to the next thing I actually remember? That's probably the fight about the dress for the funeral, which will be *days* away.

God, I hope I won't be stuck here for that long.

Dong.

I slam back into my adult body.

What's going on?

Dong.

It's the bloody meditation app. My twenty minutes of meditation are up, and it always ends on three gongs. I never understood what those were for, but now I'm wondering if it's in order to bring lost souls back to their bodies when the time is right.

I'm still sitting in my chair, facing the window. The figs are stinking up the garden. The blackbirds are singing, and the cars are humming.

My body is covered in sweat and I'm shaking. My throat feels raw. I try to say a few words, but they come out hoarse and rusty.

Feet shaking, I stand up just as the doorbell rings.

Feeling completely lost, I make it down to open the door. It's Mathilda from next door.

"Is everything all right?" she asks. "I heard screaming."

I lift a hand to my throat. "Sorry about that. I fell asleep. Bad dream."

Mathilda doesn't seem entirely convinced, but we're not really close enough for her to pry. "All right," she says. She points a finger at me. "But you come tell me if you need anything, you hear?"

I nod. "Will do, Mathilda. Thank you."

I close the front door, then just stand there looking at it for several minutes.

Five

I'M BACK IN my hometown. I told my husband I had to help out a friend, so he would take the kids after school, and just drove for three hours to get there.

I'm not in front of our old house, though. I'm on the other side of town, in a neighborhood that's very similar, except it has fences instead of hedges. The house I'm staring at is identical to all the other houses on this street, with beige plaster, white windows, and blue shutters. The mailbox is on the original side, probably homemade, and sports the name George Lambert.

My phone is in my hand, with my Dad's face staring up at me. My thumb is hovering above the call button.

Before I can decide to hit send, a car drives up behind me, and the automatic gate starts to slide open. I turn to see a white Opel idling on the street, waiting to drive into its garage.

The driver is a man in his fifties. Dark blond hair. Difficult to judge when he's sitting in his car, but he seems tall.

He turns to look at me, and I freeze as I recognize him. Same too-small nose. Same thin lips.

The passenger window lowers. "Can I help you with anything, Ma'am?"

I'm frozen in place, but after a couple of seconds I manage a tight shake of my head. My thumb is still ready to press send, though the screen has gone black.

"Well," the man—George—says. "That's my house you're staring at. If you don't have any business with me, I'd appreciate it if you'd move along."

My pulse is beating about a thousand thumps a minute and a drop of sweat trickles down between my breasts despite the cooling evening air.

"Bathroom," I blurt out.

"What?" George had started accelerating to drive his car into the garage, but the car stops after ten centimeters. He seems to study me closer, giving me a quick once-over. "I don't do bathrooms anymore," he says slowly. "Moved over to kitchens over twenty years ago."

He cocks his head and narrows his eyes. "Do I know you from somewhere, lady?"

I shake my head. I'm finally able to get my hands to work and I unlock my phone and press dial.

A car honks its horn behind me. Someone from farther down the street getting impatient with George blocking his way.

With an irritated glance behind him, George drives his Opel into the garage.

"Hey, honey," Dad says. "What's up?"

My body's frozen in place, but my voice still works. "I found him, Dad," I say. "His name is George Lambert."

Dad talks back to me, but I don't hear him. George is coming out of the garage and my first reflex is to drop my phone into my purse.

George stalks through the still-open gate and straight up to me. His face is exactly the same as I saw in my memory mere hours ago, except he's aged thirty years. A little bit of a beer gut. Less hair. But still the man who murdered my mother right in front of my eyes.

"Are you sure we've never met?" he asks. "You look familiar."

I shake my head again. "I'm sorry to have bothered you, Sir. I was just going for a walk and stopped here to check something on my phone."

His gaze never leaves my face. He chews on his lower lip as he studies me and I can practically see the gears turning in his head.

His eyes harden and his lips curl into a smirk. "You wouldn't happen to have owned a pink sun dress when you were about five?"

I can't help it; I gulp as I stare into his brown eyes. "I don't—"

"Anne, wasn't it?" He gives me a once-over, and I can't hold back the shiver that takes me over as I remember him giving my mother the exact same look. "I don't think I had the honor of learning your name face to face, but the papers were more than helpful in filling in some details."

He stares into my eyes, and although he's twenty years my senior, I'm all too aware of the fact that he's a good head taller than me. "What brings you to my door?" he asks.

"I don't know what you're—"

He grabs my elbow and steers me through the gate and toward his front door. "Why don't you come in for a cup of coffee? I believe we have some catching up to do." With one firm hand on my elbow, he uses the other to fish his keys out of his pocket while he looks up and down the street. His gaze lingers for a moment on a house a little farther down the street—the house of the man honking his horn earlier, if I wasn't mistaken.

As he opens the door, I try to break free, but he must have seen it coming. In a gesture that would probably look friendly from afar, he grabs my shoulders and pulls me inside.

Locking the door and putting the keys back in his pocket, he uses his body to force me up against the door. "How did you find me?"

My voice is shaking. "Google."

He rolls his eyes. "How did you know who to look for?"

"I saw you," I whisper.

"Of course you did." He looks like he wants to do another eye-roll but stops himself. "So after thirty years, you thought it would be time to look me up?"

My breathing is shallow and my heart threatens to jump out of my chest. "I'd like to leave now."

"Sorry," George says casually. "No can do."

He grabs the front of my shirt and pulls me behind him down a hallway.

I try to fight him, but he's so much stronger than him, I feel like I'm back in my five-year-old body.

He opens a door, and unceremoniously throws me through it.

It takes longer than expected to hit the floor—because it's not a floor, but a staircase. I tumble down, hitting my head and my hips and breaking two fingers on my left hand. At the bottom, I heave for breath and cradle my hand against my chest.

George comes down the staircase, taking his time. "Now, I'd love to do this in the kitchen," he says. "For old times' sake. But unfortunately, I'll need to clean up my mess this time, and down here is just going to be that much more practical."

Since I woke up from my meditation, I have been working mostly in a state of shock. On seeing George, I added a good dose of fear. Tumbling down the stairs, pain.

Now, as I see my mother's murderer come toward me while he rolls up the sleeves of his shirt, anger is finally making its entry.

This man destroyed my family. Ruined my childhood. Made my father into a zombie who hardly ever shakes out of his funk for long enough to come visit his grandchildren.

I am not going down without a fight.

George might think he was up against a second version of my mother. I certainly look like her. And while, physically, that might be true, there is a very important difference between today and that fateful day thirty years ago.

I don't have a child to worry about in addition to my own safety. And I know what to expect.

George talks as he takes his time on the stairs, explaining all the horrors he's going to do to me. I tune him out, having heard him say much the same things to my mother only hours earlier. Instead, I look around, searching for anything that could help me.

Six

Though I hate how vulnerable it will make me, I let George start his show without fighting back. It was what my mother had done, so I assume he won't find it surprising. When he approaches, I walk backwards until my back hits the counter of a workbench, then freeze.

He seems to want a repeat of my mother's murder—where the first order on the agenda is to remove my clothes. In my mother's case, that had meant ripping off her underwear, but for me, he'd have a little more work. He grabs my blouse at the neck and rips it open, exposing my chest to the chill cellar air.

He seems happy with what he sees and bends down to open my belt.

My mother had assumed he only had rape in mind when he started, not murder. And she had me to look out for. So she'd let him do whatever he wanted. When she realized how far he'd go, it was too late.

I know where this is going from the start, and my kids are safe with their father hundreds of kilometers away.

I lean back and stretch my hand toward the rack above the workbench. I grab whatever I touch first and barely have the time to register that it's a huge wrench before slamming it down on George's head.

He crumples at my feet, blood oozing from a wound just above his ear.

I don't even bother to check if he's breathing, I just run for the stairs.

The door's locked. I try to force it open, but I don't have the necessary body weight. Just as I consider the possibility of going back down to look for my purse—which I must have lost at some point during my fall down the stairs—I hear sirens.

SEVEN

I SIT IN the back of an ambulance, letting medical personnel look after my broken fingers, when they bring George out of the house. The left half of his face is covered in blood, but he's walking on his own and his eyes are locked on mine for the entire walk between his front door and the waiting police car.

With my uninjured right hand, I hold my phone to my ear and listen to my father's voice. He'd kept the connected call on his cell phone while using the land line to call the police. Somehow, he'd understood that something very bad was happening and sent the police after the name I gave him.

"How long have you known?" he asks me. His voice is shaky.

"Just a few hours, Dad," I reply. "I only discovered the memory this afternoon."

He's silent for a moment. "Everything?"

I close my eyes. "Yes. But he'll be going to prison now. Mom will finally get justice."

We sit in silence, enjoying the cool evening in two different cities.

"Maybe I could come visit this weekend," Dad says. "I haven't seen the kids in a while."

"That'd be great, Dad."

Thank You

THANK YOU FOR reading *Hidden Horros*. I hope you enjoyed it!

I certainly freaked myself out writing it... I had this whole plan for where the character should end up when she meditated. It was going to be fantasy and fun.

Needless to say, the muse went elsewhere. And I'm happy it did!

If you liked the story, you might want to check out some of my other books mentioned on the next page. It's mostly Mysteries, but a few Science Fiction short stories will pop up, too.

And don't forget that the first book of my *Tolosa Mystery* series, *The Red Brick Haze*, is available for free on my website.

R.W. Wallace
www.rwwallace.com

Also by R.W. Wallace

Mystery

THE TOLOSA MYSTERY SERIES
The Red Brick Haze (free)
The Red Brick Cellars
The Red Brick Basilica

GHOST DETECTIVE SHORTS (COMING SOON)
Just Desserts
Lost Friends
Family Bonds
Till Death
Family History
Common Ground
Heritage
Eternal Bond
New Beginnings

SHORT STORIES
Cold Blue Eternity
Hidden Horrors
Critters
Gertrude and the Trojan Horse
First Impressions
Let Them Eat Cake
Out of Sight
Two's Company
Like Mother Like Daughter

Fantasy (Short Stories)
Unexpected Consequences
Morbier Impossible
A Second Chance

Science Fiction (Short Stories)
The Vanguard

Lollapalooza Shorts
Quarantine
Common Enemies
Coiled Danger
Mars Meeting

Adventure (Short Stories)
Size Matters

www.ingramcontent.com/pod-product-compliance
Lightning Source LLC
LaVergne TN
LVHW051922060526
838201LV00060B/4143